Footprints
in the Snow

First published in 2010
by Wayland

Text copyright © Karen Wallace
Illustration copyright © Jackie Harland

Wayland
338 Euston Road
London NW1 3BH

Wayland Australia
Level 17/207 Kent Street
Sydney, NSW 2000

Series Editor: Louise John
Editor: Katie Powell
Cover design: Paul Cherrill
Design: D.R.ink
Consultant: Shirley Bickler

A CIP catalogue record for this book is available from the British Library.

ISBN 9780750263382

Printed in China

Wayland is a division of Hachette Children's Books,
an Hachette UK Company

www.hachette.co.uk

Footprints in the Snow

Written by Karen Wallace
Illustrated by Jackie Harland

WAYLAND

It was winter on the farm.
When the snow began to fall,
all the animals huddled
together in the barn.

The next day, Cow woke
up and looked out over
the fields.

"Who made those footprints in the snow," she mooed.

"Maybe it was a fox,"
said Cat.

"No, those footprints are too big," said Cow.

"Maybe it was a wolf!"
said Horse.

"Or a monster snowman,"
said Sheep. She was
shaking like jelly.
"I don't like monsters."

"There's no such thing as a monster snowman," said Dog.

"But look! The footprints are everywhere," said Sheep.

"Please help catch the
monster, Detective Dog,"
said Cat. "We're scared."

"Don't worry, Cat. I'll find
out who left those footprints,"
said Dog.

But, that day, Cow stopped making milk...

Hen stopped laying eggs...

...and Cat stopped
catching mice.

All the animals were
too scared.

Rabbit hid in her burrow
and didn't come out.

Even Horse and Sheep were
too scared to eat!

The farmer was not happy.
His farm was upside down
and he didn't know what
to do.

"What is wrong with the animals?" he asked Dog.

That night, Dog kept watch.
In the morning, he saw the
farmer go out into the field.

Dog followed him.

Dog watched as the farmer
put on some strange shoes
and began to walk on
the snow.

Dog went to have a closer
look. The strange shoes
were making the very
large footprints!

Detective Dog raced back
to the farm.

"It's the farmer's shoes!" he cried. "He's got snow shoes so that he can walk on the snow. There's no monster snowman at all!"

"Well done, Dog!" cried the animals. "You're the best detective in the world!"

That day, Hen laid an egg, Cat caught a mouse and Cow made lots of milk.

Best of all, the farmer was happy again. He had an egg for his breakfast and milk in his tea!

Hurray for Detective Dog!

START READING is a series of highly enjoyable books for beginner readers. **The books have been carefully graded to match the Book Bands widely used in schools.** This enables readers to be sure they choose books that match their own reading ability.

Look out for the Band colour on the book in our Start Reading logo.

The Bands are:

Pink Band 1A & 1B

Red Band 2

Yellow Band 3

Blue Band 4

Green Band 5

Orange Band 6

Turquoise Band 7

Purple Band 8

Gold Band 9

START READING books can be read independently or shared with an adult. They promote the enjoyment of reading through satisfying stories supported by fun illustrations.

Karen Wallace was brought up in a log cabin in Canada. She has written lots of different books for children and even won a few awards. Karen likes writing funny books because she can laugh at her own jokes! She has two sons and two cats.

Jackie Harland is woken up every morning by her two cats taking it in turns to nibble her toes and pat her face with their paws. It works every time, and they always get their breakfast first. In spite of that, she loves them very much, and after she finally gets to eat her own breakfast, she loves painting, especially animals.